Beauty and the Beast

A Book to Read and Color

Adapted by
Suzanne Gruber

Illustrated by
Laurie A. Struck

Watermill Press

Once upon a time, there was a rich merchant...

...who had three daughters.

The youngest daughter was called Beauty,
because she was the kindest and most
beautiful of the three.

Soon, bad luck came to the merchant.
He had to move his family to
a poor house in the country.

Beauty worked very hard...

...while her sisters did nothing.

One day, the merchant went away on a trip.
"What presents shall I bring back?" he asked his
daughters. The two oldest daughters asked him for
dresses. But Beauty asked only for a rose.

On his way home, the merchant
got lost in the forest.

He soon came to a large palace,
and went inside.

Although no one seemed to be
home, there was food on the table.
So the merchant ate the food and
fell fast asleep.

In the morning, the merchant wandered into the
garden. There, he picked a rose for Beauty.

Suddenly, he heard a strange noise. He turned and saw a terrible beast!

"You must die for stealing my roses!" the Beast cried.

The merchant told the Beast that he picked the rose for one of his three daughters.

"I will let you live if one of your daughters comes here to take your place," the Beast replied.

When the merchant got home, he told his
daughters about his promise to the Beast.

"I will go," said Beauty, "for I do not
want you to be killed by the Beast."

The merchant took Beauty to the Beast's palace,
where she was treated very kindly.

The Beast gave her beautiful dresses,
jewels and fine meals. He even gave her a
magic mirror so she could see her father!

Each day, the Beast asked Beauty
if she would marry him.
But each day, she
told him no.

"It is a shame
that he is so ugly,"
she thought, "for
he is so kind
and gentle."

One day, Beauty looked
into her magic mirror
and saw that her father
was very sick.

The Beast said, "You are free to go home.
But promise me you will return in eight
days. If you do not return,
I shall die."

When Beauty had promised, the
Beast gave her a magic ring that
took her home to her father.

Soon, Beauty's father was well. But her sisters asked her to stay longer than eight days.

One night, Beauty dreamed that the Beast was dying because she had broken her promise to him.

So Beauty used
the magic ring
to return to the
Beast's palace.

She found the Beast
lying in the garden.

"You must not die, Beast!" she cried.
"You must live,
so we can
be married!"

Suddenly, Beauty saw fireworks bursting over the garden.

When she turned back
to the Beast, she
saw a handsome
prince. "Where is
my Beast?" she cried.

"I was the Beast," the prince answered.
"But you have broken the magical
spell by loving me."

And so they were married, and
lived happily ever after.